Let's Doodle, Otis!

#1 *New York Times* Bestselling

Loren Long

Grosset & Dunlap
An Imprint of Penguin Group (USA) LLC

penguin.com
A Penguin Random House Company

ISBN 978-0-448-48405-1

10 9 8 7 6 5 4 3 2 1

Putt puff puttedy chuff! Otis and his farmer work together to take care of the farm they call home. Can you add the rolling hills of the farm to the scene?

After working hard all day, Otis loves to play.
Draw the bales of hay that Otis is jumping over.

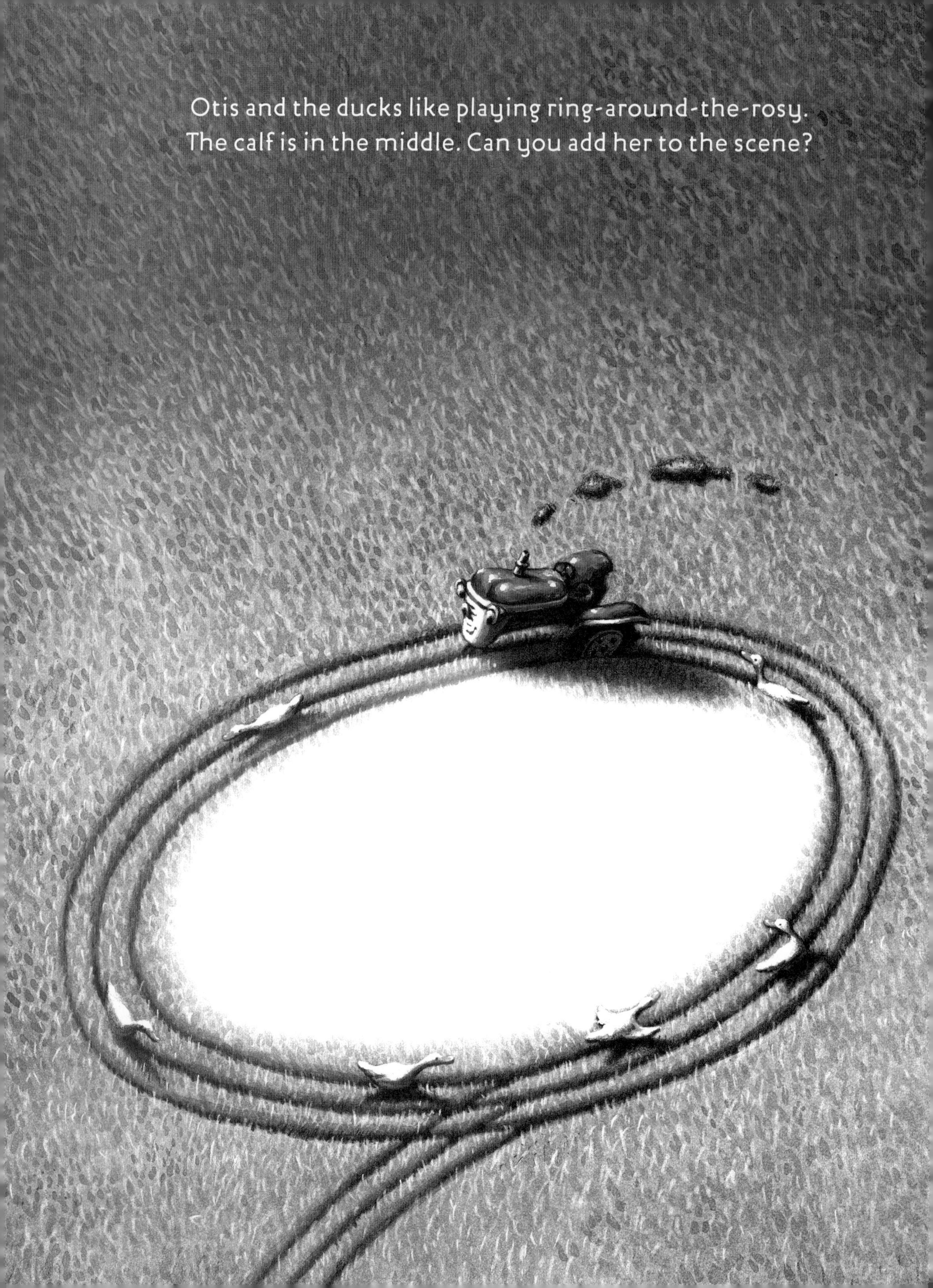

Otis and the ducks like playing ring-around-the-rosy.
The calf is in the middle. Can you add her to the scene?

Every night, tired and happy Otis putt-puffs
into the barn for a good night's sleep.
Can you draw the barn where Otis sleeps?

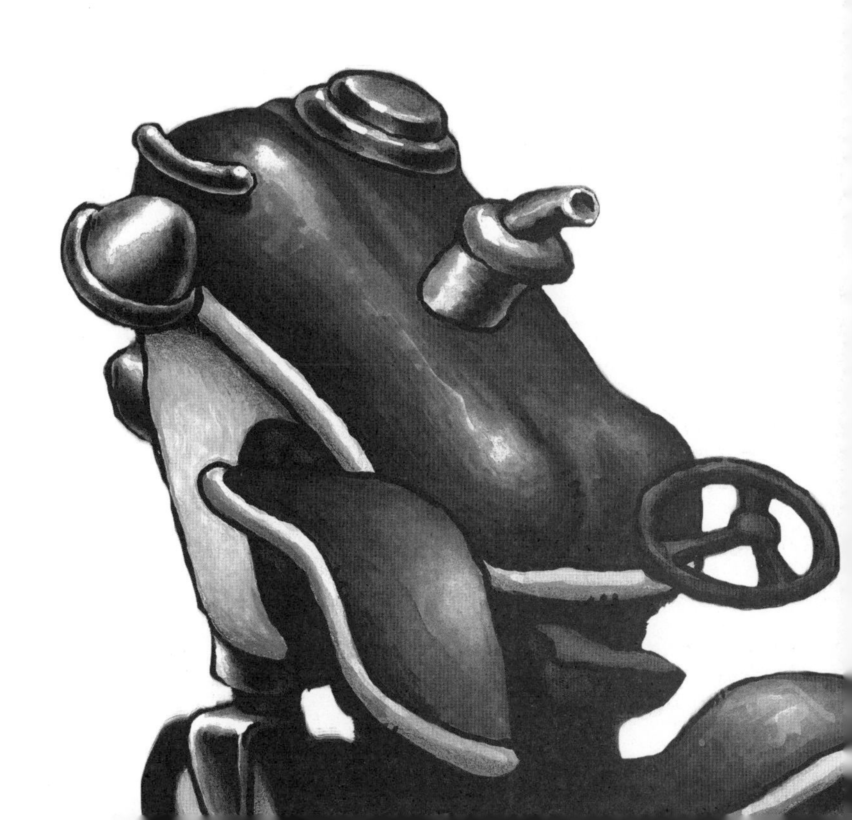

Otis and the calf like to sit under the apple tree and watch the farm.
Draw the calf and the apple tree.

Otis had to move out of the barn when the farmer bought a brand-new yellow tractor. Can you add the big yellow tractor to the scene?

Otis saved the calf from Mud Pond!
The two of them are leading the townspeople, the fire truck, and the big yellow tractor in a parade.
Can you draw the parade?

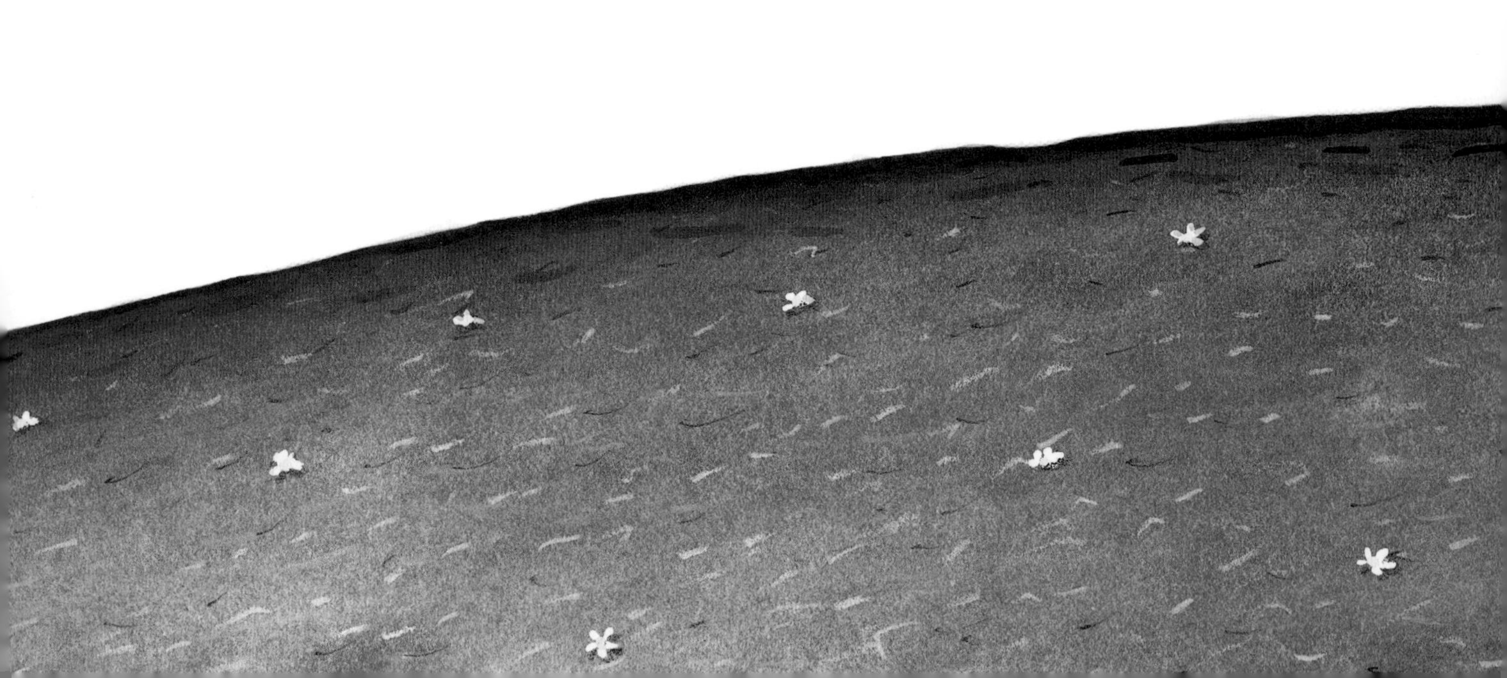

Otis and the puppy love to play together on the farm.
Otis drives over the rolling hills, and the puppy sits happily on top of Otis.
Can you draw the puppy?

Otis and the puppy are playing hide-and-seek, but the puppy is chasing a butterfly instead. Can you draw the butterfly?

After a long day of playing,
the puppy likes to curl up and fall asleep on Otis.
Add the sleeping puppy to the scene.

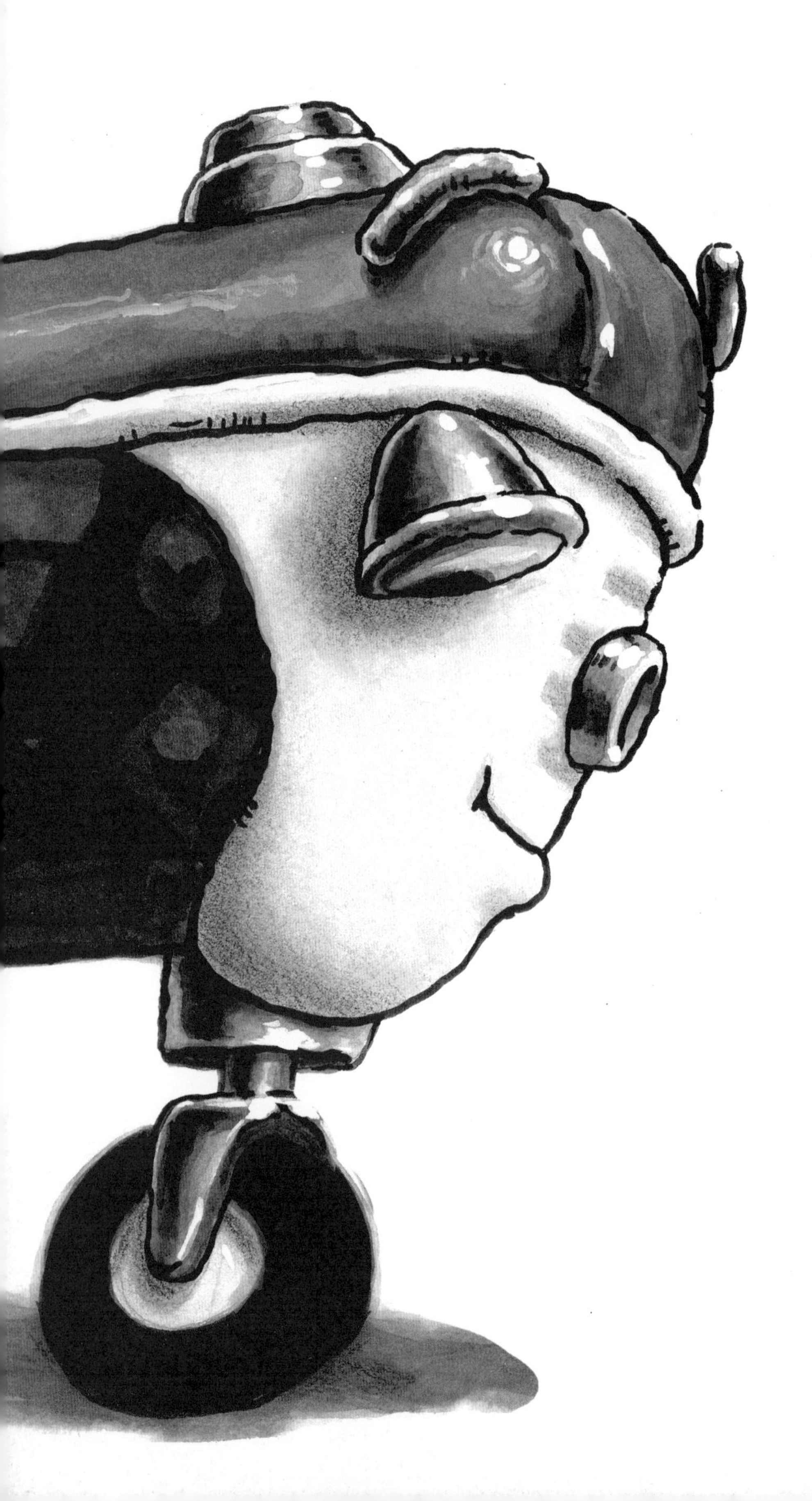

Otis is working very hard to pull a tree stump out of the ground. *Putt puff puttedy chuff!* Can you draw the tree stump Otis is pulling?

The farmer has a brand-new yellow tractor, so Otis has to stay outside.
The weeds are beginning to cover his tires.
Draw the calf walking up the hill to visit Otis.

Of all the animals on the farm, the bull is definitely the biggest.
It has long horns, big hooves, and a swishy tail.
Can you draw a bull in the space below?

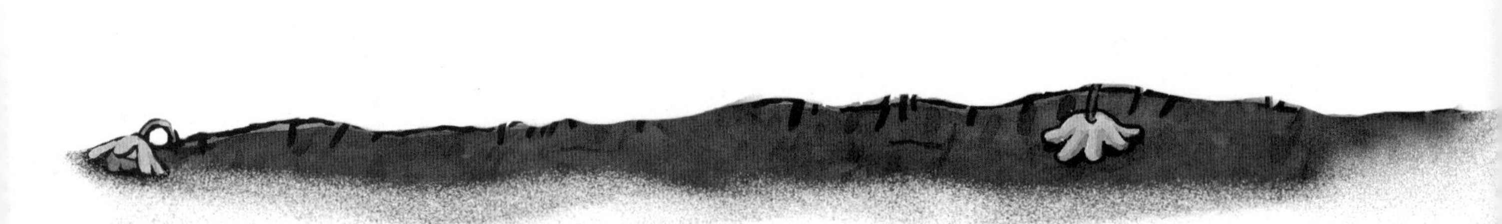

Oh no—the calf is stuck in a pool of mud!
The farmer is trying to pull the calf to safety.
Draw the farmer pulling on the rope in the picture below.

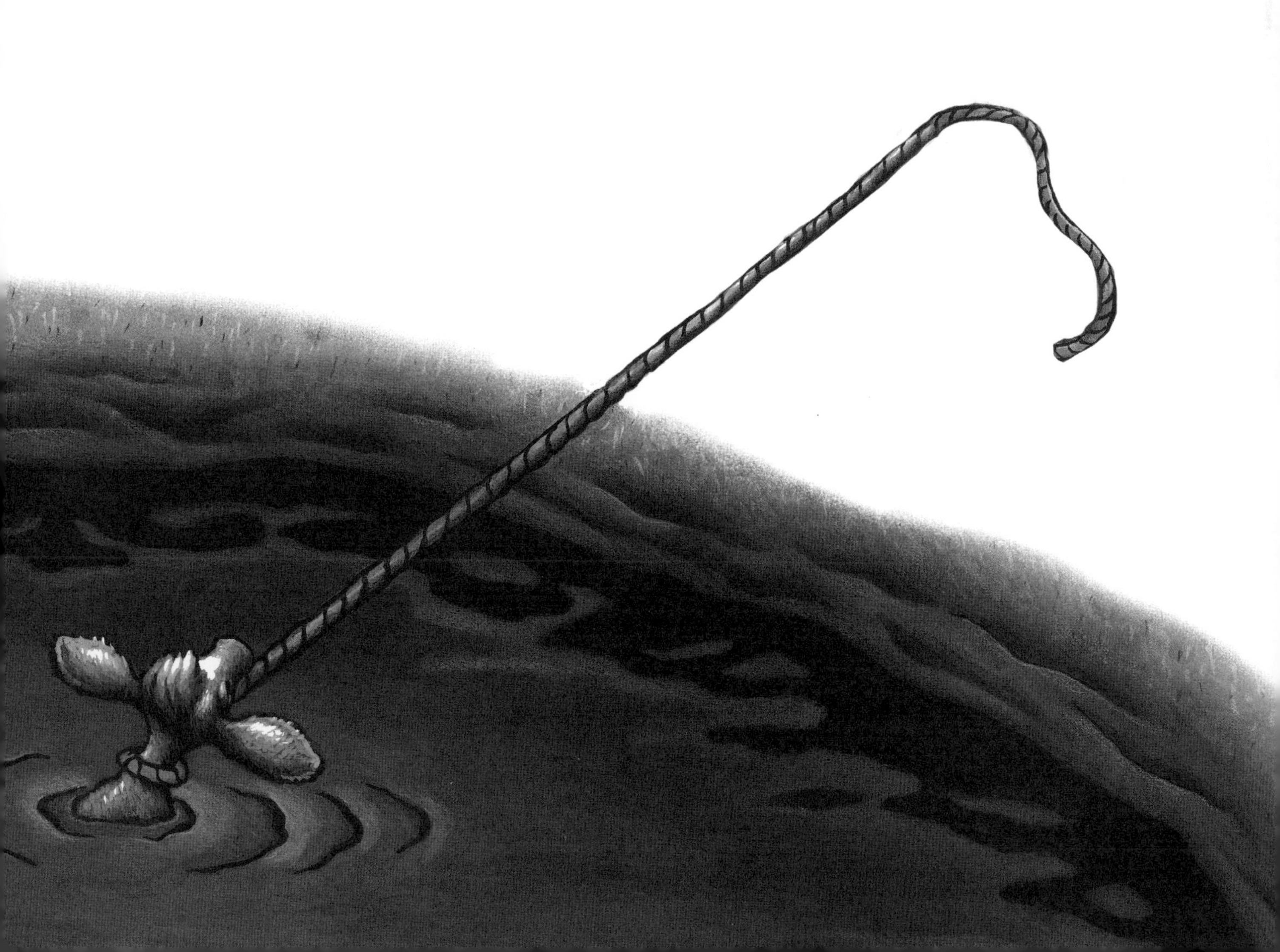

The bull doesn't seem to like any of the other animals on the farm—
he snorts, snarls, and flares his nostrils, and everyone is afraid of him!
Draw the horse and cow running away from the bull.

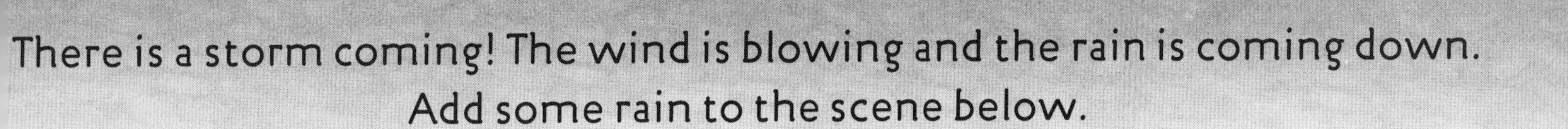

There is a storm coming! The wind is blowing and the rain is coming down.
Add some rain to the scene below.

Some firemen have come to help pull the calf out of Mud Pond.
Add the fire engine to the picture below.

There are dark storm clouds in the sky, and the tornado has already reached the hills in the distance.
Can you draw the tornado?

Otis wants to make friends with the bull, so he takes him a shiny red apple. The bull doesn't want it—he charges right at the fence! Draw Otis and the shiny red apple as it flies through the air.

Otis is coming to save the calf from being stuck in Mud Pond! Draw Otis driving down the hill—*putt puff puttedy chuff*—to save his friend.

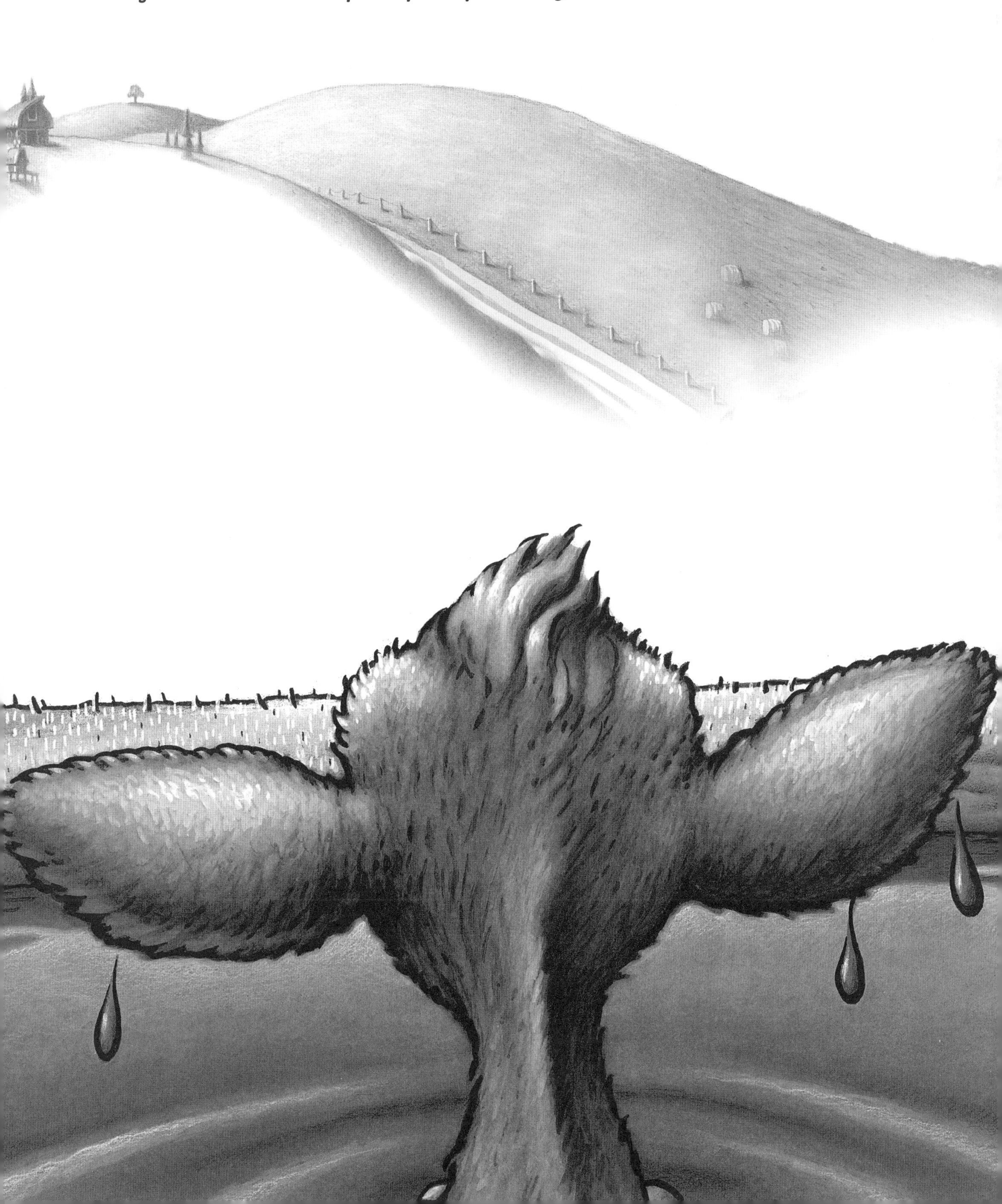

Otis, the horse, the cow, and the calf like to play follow-the-leader.
Can you add them playing to the scene below?

The farmer has given Otis a brand-new horn.
Draw the shiny new horn in the farmer's hand.

The other animals are very excited about
the brand-new addition to the farm—
a beautiful baby foal.
Draw the foal in the scene below.

The tornado has passed, and it caused a lot of damage. Trees have fallen over, the barn was torn down, and the bullpen is now a pile of logs. Finish the scene in the space below.

It's Christmastime, and Otis and the animals are watching the farmer decorate a Christmas tree. Can you draw the tree?

Otis, the calf, and the puppy are going for a cold drive in the snow.
Can you draw in the tracks they have left behind them?

Otis and his animal friends are taking cover from a big storm.
The wind is blowing hard, and there are leaves flying everywhere.
Add the leaves to the scene below.

Otis is lost in the snow! Draw Otis as he *very carefully* makes his way down the snow-covered log.

Otis loves all the animals on the farm!
Draw the horse, bull, calf, and ducks
as they all walk together with Otis.